Creepy Crawly Calypso

To Phili... 2020

Love

uncle
Gus
xx

For Mercedes, who counts — T. L.
For Matthew — D. H.

Barefoot Books
294 Banbury Road
Oxford, OX2 7ED

Text copyright © 2004 by Tony Langham
Illustrations copyright © 2004 by Debbie Harter
The moral rights of Tony Langham and Debbie Harter have been asserted
Performed by Richard Love (lead vocal and congas), Mark Collins (piano),
Alex Hutchings (guitar and saxophone) and Panache (steel pan band)
Musical composition and arrangement © 2004 by Mark Collins, newSense Music Productions
Recorded, mixed and mastered by Valley Recordings, England
Animation by Karrot Animation, London

First published in Great Britain by Barefoot Books, Ltd in 2004
The paperback edition with enhanced CD first published in 2012

Graphic design by Barefoot Books, Oxford
Colour separation by Grafiscan, Verona
Printed in China on 100% acid-free paper
This book was typeset in Mercurius Medium
The illustrations were prepared in watercolour, pen and ink, and crayon on thick watercolour paper

ISBN 978-1-84686-827-6

British Cataloguing-in-Publication Data:
a catalogue record for this book is available from the British Library

3 5 7 9 8 6 4

Creepy Crawly Calypso

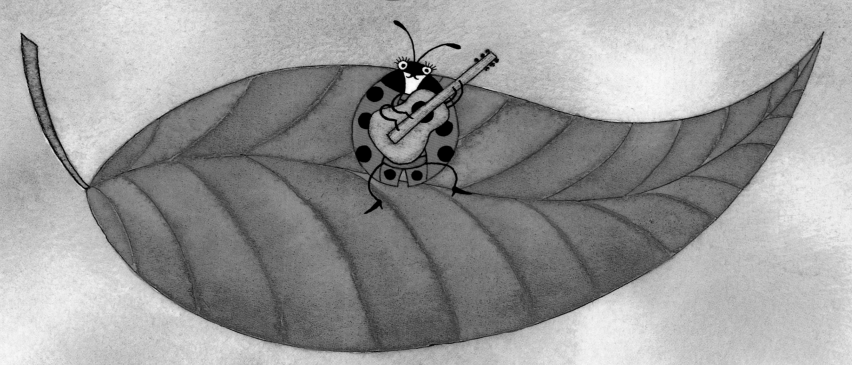

Written by **Tony Langham**
Illustrated by **Debbie Harter**
Sung by **Richard Love**

Barefoot Books
Step inside a story

If you like good music,
if you want a treat,
just hear these creepy crawlies
play their cool calypso beat!

2 **Second come the butterflies, with accordions.**

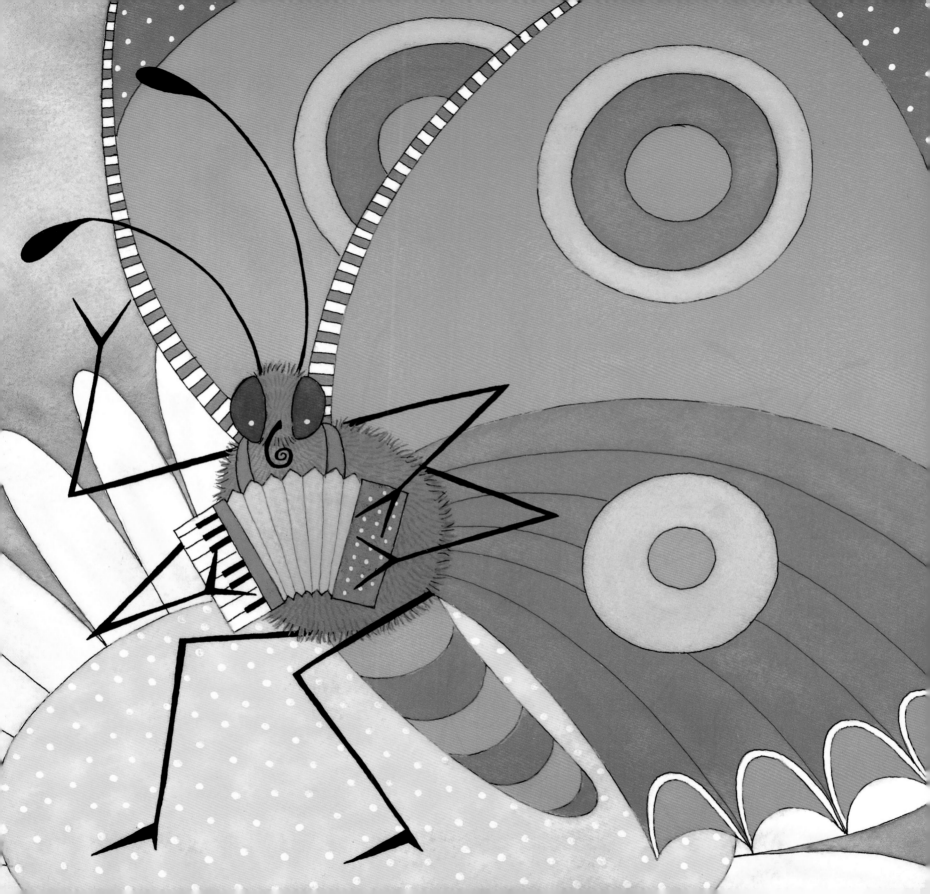

3 Third come the cockroaches, playing saxophones.

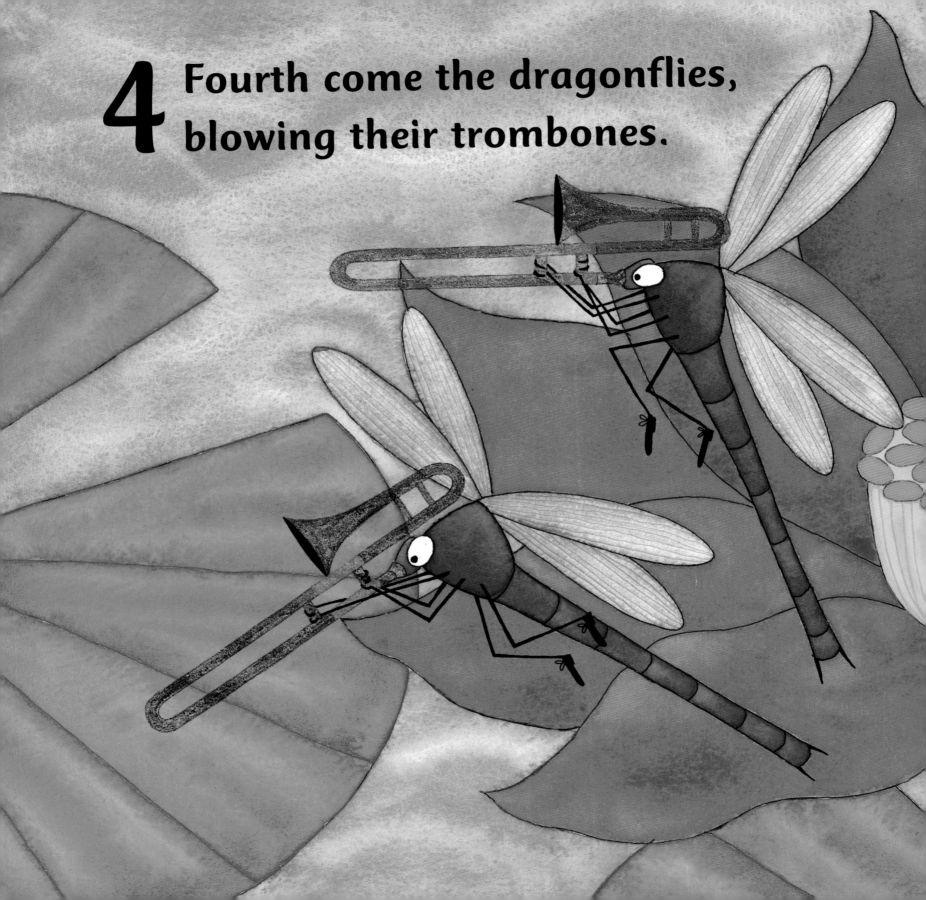

4 Fourth come the dragonflies,
blowing their trombones.

5 Fifth come the fireflies,
with brass trumpets to toot.

6 Sixth come the army ants, bearing tiny flutes.

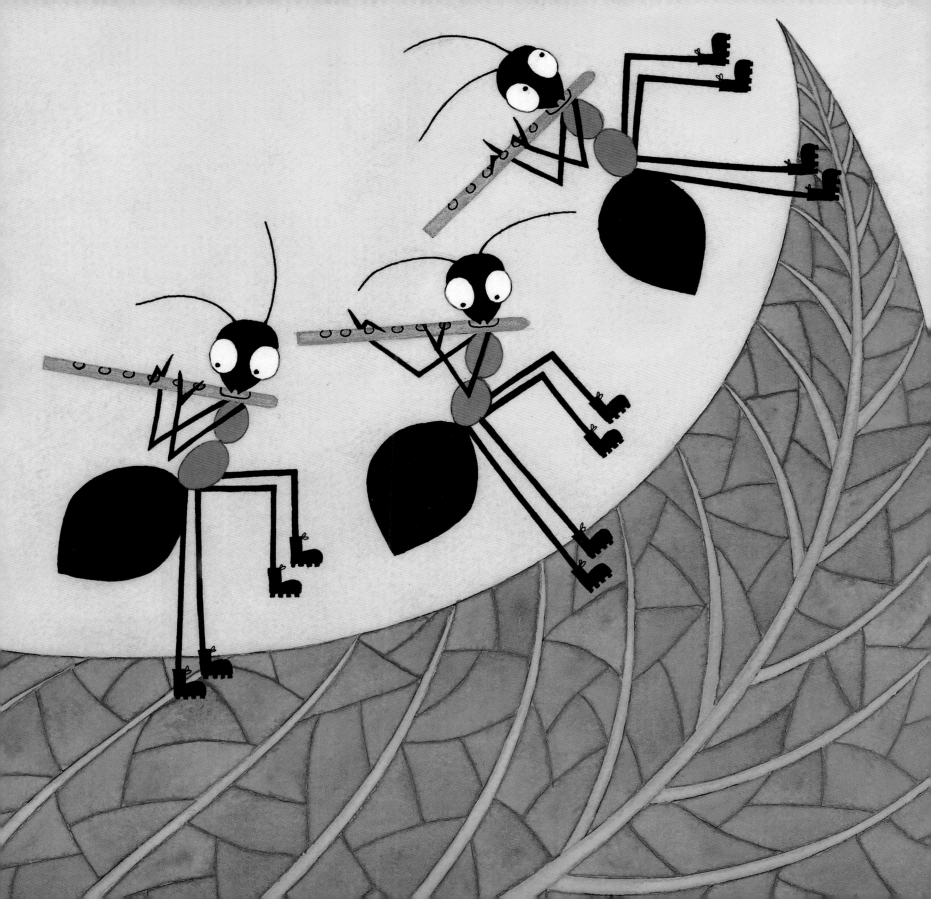

7 Seventh come the ladybirds, strumming their guitars.

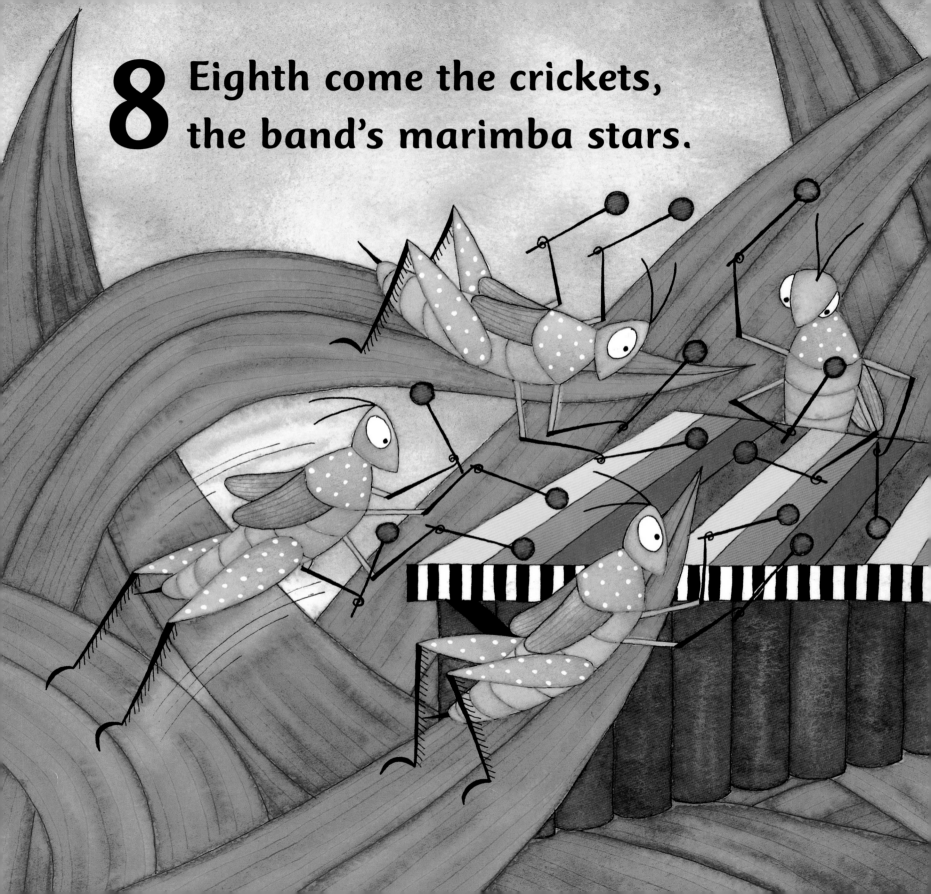

8 Eighth come the crickets, the band's marimba stars.

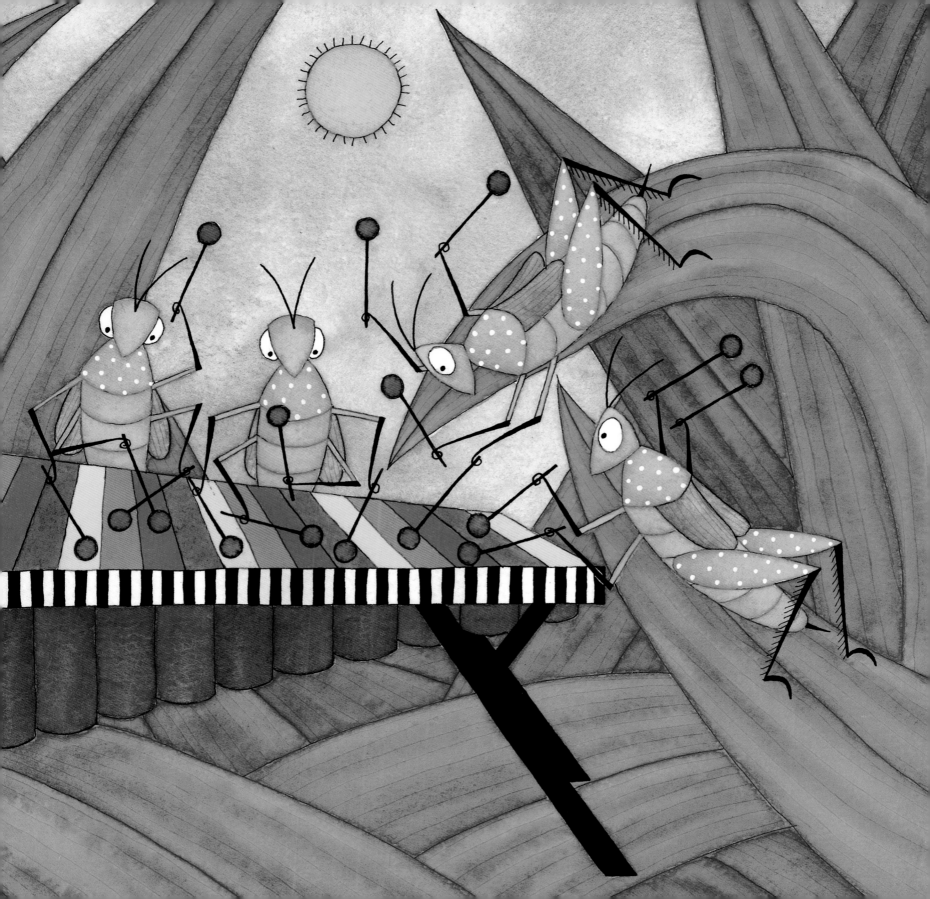

9 Ninth come the beetles, beating congas loudly.

10 Tenth come the centipedes, tinkling pianos proudly.

For any kind of party,
at any time of day,
the creepy crawly calypso
is the best music to play!

Calypso Bands

Calypso bands come from the West Indies. The musicians play many kinds of instruments and sing lively, bouncy songs, often about island characters or events. All of the instruments in this book are played in calypso bands.

Accordion
An accordion is played by being squeezed in and out. Pulling it out fills it with air, and pushing it in forces the air out. Pressing the keys while the air goes out makes different notes.

Steel Drums
These are metal drums made from empty oil-drums. Drums were banned in Trinidad in the 1930s, so the local people created their own musical drums out of whatever objects they could find. Steel drums are also called steel pans.

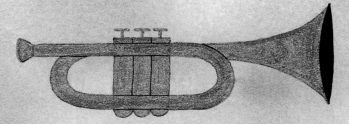

Trombone
The trombone is a long brass instrument. It has a large bell shape at one end and a moving part that slides up and down. The player blows into the mouthpiece and makes different notes by moving the slider. The trombone makes a deep, rich noise.

Saxophone
The saxophone was invented by a Belgian man called Adolphe Sax. The saxophone is usually made of metal and has lots of keys that help to produce the different notes while the player blows into it.

Trumpet
This is another brass instrument with a bell-shaped end where the sound comes out, a bit like a trombone. But trumpets are smaller and higher-pitched, and the player makes notes by pressing down three keys (these are called valves).

Flute

A flute is a long metal tube with holes all along it. The player blows over a hole at one end to create sound. He makes different notes by opening and closing the keys with his fingers. The notes made by a flute are delicate and soft.

Spanish Guitar

Spanish guitars are made of wood and have six nylon strings. The different notes are produced by pressing the strings with one hand and plucking or strumming with the other.

Marimba

A marimba is a type of xylophone which is played with a small wooden striker. The player hits wooden rectangles of different lengths to make a range of notes. The marimba is a descendant of the very first musical instrument ever created.

Conga Drum

A conga drum is a long, upright drum made from wood — the earliest congas were made out of hollowed-out logs. The skin that is stretched across the top of the drum is made out of animal hide or plastic, and can be tightened and loosened to make different notes.

Piano

A piano has eighty-eight black and white keys. When you play them, the keys make small hammers inside the piano hit steel strings. All the strings are different thicknesses and lengths, which makes them each produce a different note.

The Creepy Crawlies

Tarantula
Tarantulas are large, hairy spiders. Some tarantulas are poisonous and can give nasty bites. They have eight eyes, and some female tarantulas can live for as long as thirty years.

Butterfly
Butterflies are beautiful flying insects with long, slender bodies and four fragile, often highly coloured and patterned wings. Butterflies hear sounds through their wings.

Cockroach
Cockroaches are active at night, and most of them are omnivorous (which means they will eat anything and everything!). Some cockroaches can fly.

Dragonfly
Dragonflies are flying insects with long thin bodies and transparent wings. Their bodies can be all the colours of the rainbow. They often live near rivers, streams and ponds.

Firefly
Fireflies are flying beetles which come out at night. They have glowing chemicals in their tummies which can flash on and off, to show where they are and attract mates.

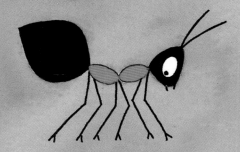

Ant
Ants are social insects that usually live in large colonies. Ants build large nests, which are ruled by a Queen Ant. Ants work as teams for the good of each colony.

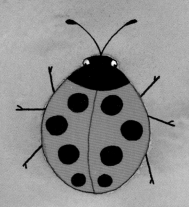

Ladybird
Ladybirds are usually red or yellow with black spots, or else black with red or yellow spots. Different types of ladybird have different numbers of spots. Their bright colours help to scare away animals that want to eat them.

Cricket
Crickets are insects with long back legs and long antennae or 'feelers'. The males make a chirping sound by rubbing their back legs together. This is how they 'sing' and attract female crickets.

Beetle
Beetles are insects which come in many sizes, shapes and colours. They may crawl or fly or do both. There are over 300,000 different types of beetle in the world.

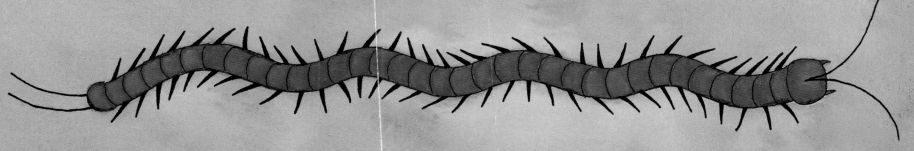

Centipede
Centipedes are worm-like creatures with segmented bodies, each segment carrying a pair of legs. Centipedes are supposed to have a hundred feet. Count them and see if it's true!

The Creepy Crawly Calypso!